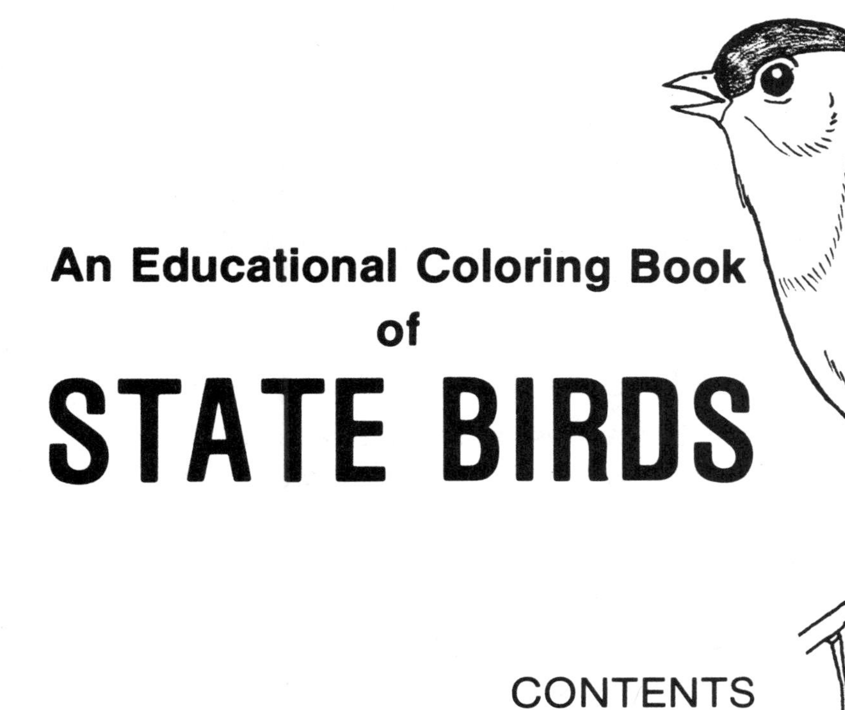

An Educational Coloring Book of STATE BIRDS

CONTENTS

EDITOR
Linda Spizzirri

ASST. EDITOR
Jacqueline Sontheimer

ILLUSTRATION
Peter M. Spizzirri

COVER ART
Peter M. Spizzirri

An Educational Coloring Book of STATE BIRDS • Published by SPIZZIRRI PUBLISHING, INC., P.O. BOX 9397, RAPID CITY, SOUTH DAKOTÁ 57709.
Printed in U.S.A.

Each state in the United States has chosen its favorite bird to be its state bird. Often several states have chosen the same bird as their favorite, so there are only 28 different state birds. You will find each of them illustrated in this book. Besides the 28 state birds, you will also find the bald eagle illustrated, which is the national bird of the United States of America.

COLORING INSTRUCTIONS

The diagram below shows a bird with its various body parts labeled. The diagram is given, both as a learning tool and as a coloring reference aid. Because many birds have different colors on the various parts of their bodies, coloring instructions in this book are given in reference to the different parts as given in the diagram. Not all of our state birds are brightly colored or even multi-colored. When this is the case, the coloring instructions will simply indicate that the entire body, upper body or wing are of a single color.

Patterns are indicated, plus some light shading is given, to help you to color these lovely state birds in a realistic manner.

Most people know what the state bird of their own state is. We hope this book serves as a fun learning experience, to find out the state birds of all 50 states and to enjoy coloring them.

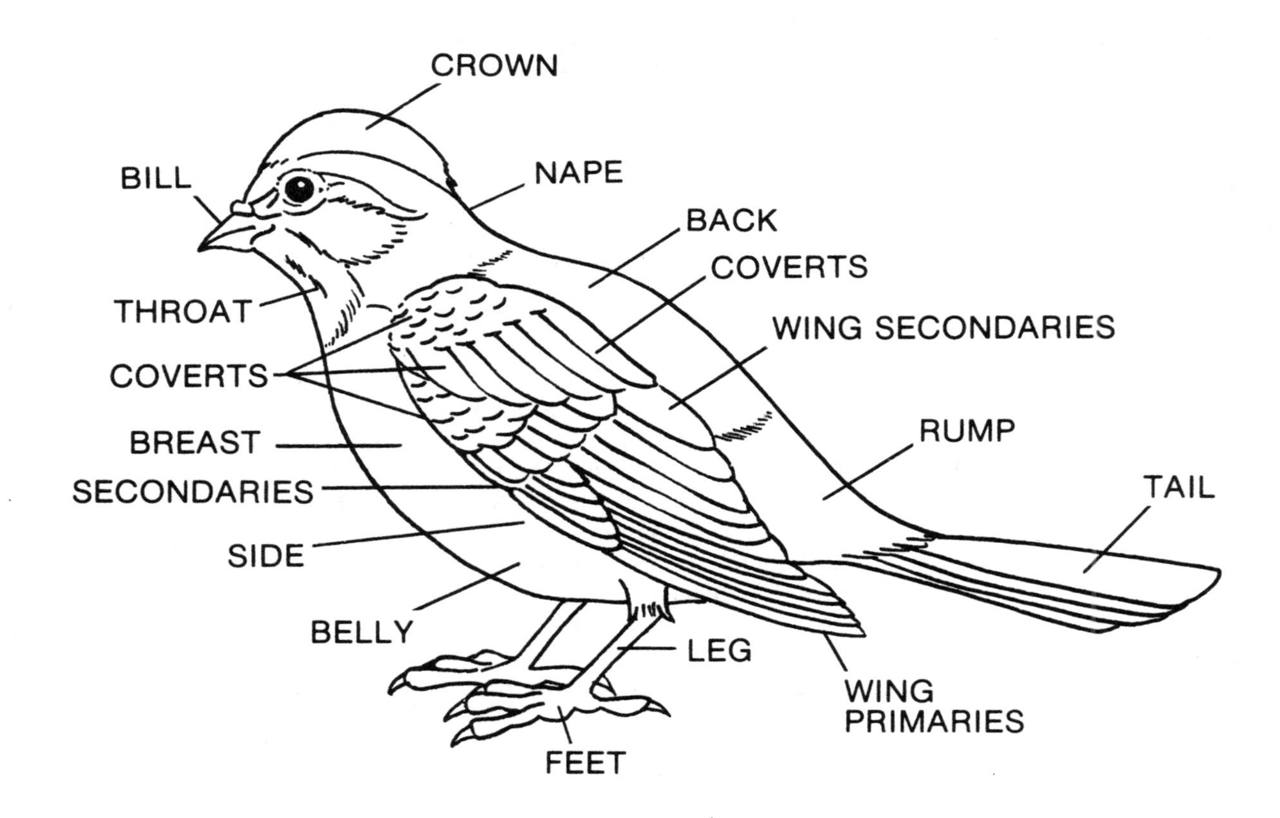

NAME: CAROLINA WREN (*Thryothorus ludovicianus*)
STATE BIRD OF: SOUTH CAROLINA
COLOR IT: White eye stripe and throat, tan sides. Red-brown upper head, wings, back & tail with black pattern.

NAME: PURPLE FINCH (*Carpodacus purpureus*)
STATE BIRD OF: NEW HAMPSHIRE
COLOR IT: Raspberry-red head, upper body, wings & tail. Raspberry spotted breast, white belly.

NAME: GOLDFINCH (*Carduelis tristis*)
STATE BIRD OF: IOWA, NEW JERSEY, WASHINGTON
COLOR IT: Black crown, white rump, yellow back, breast and belly. Black wings and tail with white pattern stripes.

NAME: LARK BUNTING (*Calamospiza melanocorys*)
STATE BIRD OF: COLORADO
COLOR IT: Black or dark gray with white wing patches.

NAME: HERMIT THRUSH (*Catharus guttatus*)
STATE BIRD OF: VERMONT
COLOR IT: Brown upper body, reddish brown rump and tail. White throat and breast with brown spots, white belly.

NAME: BLACK CAPPED CHICKADEE (*Parus atricapillus*)
STATE BIRD OF: MAINE, MASSACHUSETTS
COLOR IT: Black crown, nape and throat, white cheek. Light gray body below, dark gray upper body and tail.

NAME: MOUNTAIN BLUEBIRD (*Sialia currucoides*)
STATE BIRD OF: IDAHO, NEVADA
COLOR IT: Sky blue upper body and head, light blue throat, breast and belly. Dark gray beak, legs and feet.

NAME: CARDINAL (*Cardinalis cardinalis*)
STATE BIRD OF: ILLINOIS, INDIANA, KENTUCKY, NORTH CAROLINA, OHIO, VIRGINIA, WEST VIRGINIA
COLOR IT: Red body and beak, black around eye and black throat patch.

NAME: COMMON FLICKER (*Colaptes auratus*)
STATE BIRD OF: ALABAMA
COLOR IT: Gray crown and nape with red patch. Black "mustache" and throat patch, tan cheeks and throat. Light tan breast and belly with brown spots. Brown back, wings and tail, yellow under wings and tail.

NAME: BROWN THRASHER (*Toxostoma rufum*)
STATE BIRD OF: GEORGIA
COLOR IT: Reddish brown upper body, head, wings and tail. White throat, breast, tips on coverts, white belly with brown spots.

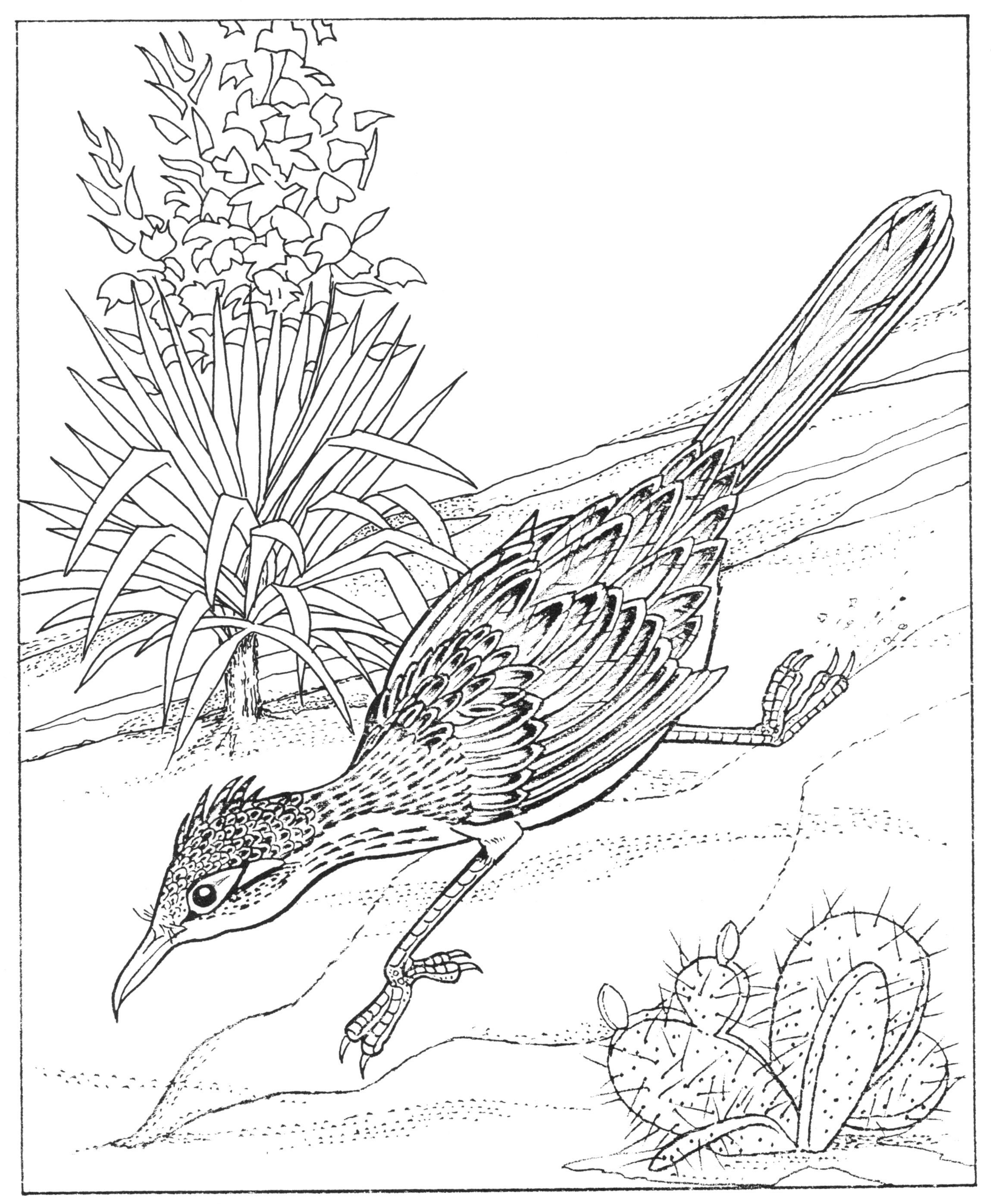

NAME: ROADRUNNER (*Geococcyx californianus*)
STATE BIRD OF: NEW MEXICO
COLOR IT: Blue eye patch, red patch over cheek. Grayish brown head, upper half, wings and tail with a darker brown pattern. Light brown upper feather tips, light tan belly and neck. Light tan breast with brown spot pattern.

NAME: BALTIMORE ORIOLE (*Icterus galbula*)
STATE BIRD OF: MARYLAND
COLOR IT: Orange rump, wing patch, breast and belly. Black head, nape, throat and back. Black wing with white tips, black tail with orange mixture.

NAME: EASTERN BLUE BIRD (*Sialia sialis*)
STATE BIRD OF: MISSOURI, NEW YORK
COLOR IT: Bright blue upper body, head, wings and tail, orange-red throat and breast, white belly.

NAME: SCISSOR-TAILED FLYCATCHER (*Muscivora forficata*)
STATE BIRD OF: OKLAHOMA
COLOR IT: Light gray head, throat, back and wing patches. Dark gray wings with white tips, dark gray tail with light gray tips and white patches. Pink belly flanks.

NAME: WESTERN MEADOWLARK (*Sturnella neglecta*)
STATE BIRD OF: KANSAS, MONTANA, NEBRASKA, NORTH DAKOTA, OREGON, WYOMING
COLOR IT: Yellow eye stripe, throat, breast and belly. Brown crown, nape and wings. Black patch under throat. White sides and under tail with brown spots.

NAME: CACTUS WREN (*Campylorhynchus brunneicapillus*)
STATE BIRD OF: ARIZONA
COLOR IT: White eye stripe. Brown head, back, rump, tail and wings with black bars. White throat, breast and belly with black spots.

NAME: MOCKING BIRD (*Mimus polyglottos*)

STATE BIRD OF: ARKANSAS, FLORIDA, MISSISSIPPI, TENNESSEE, TEXAS

COLOR IT: Gray upper body, dark gray tail with white edges on feathers. Gray-black wings with white tips on coverts, white patch on front secondaries, white throat and belly.

NAME: BLUE HEN CHICKEN (*Gallus gallus*)
STATE BIRD OF: DELAWARE
COLOR IT: Gray body, legs, feet and bill with red wattle and comb.

NAME: RHODE ISLAND RED (*Gallus gallus*)
STATE BIRD OF: RHODE ISLAND
COLOR IT: Red-brown body with black tail feather. Red wattle and comb, yellow-brown bill, legs and feet.

NAME: CALIFORNIA QUAIL (*Lophortyx californicus*)
STATE BIRD OF: CALIFORNIA
COLOR IT: Black plume on head, brown crown, white streak over eye and below throat. Black-brown throat, brown back and wings. Brown sides with white streaks. Gray nape, breast and tail. Brown and white scale pattern on belly.

NAME: RING-NECKED PHEASANT (*Phasianus colchicus*)
STATE BIRD OF: SOUTH DAKOTA
COLOR IT: MALE - Green head with red cheeks, white ring around neck, gray coverts and rump. Red-brown body with dark brown-black pattern, lighter brown wings with white pattern, dark brown pattern tail. FEMALE - Brown with dark brown pattern.

NAME: CALIFORNIA GULL (*Larus californicus*)
STATE BIRD OF: UTAH
COLOR IT: White head, neck, breast and belly, yellow beak, legs and feet, black tail. Gray back, rump and wings with white and black patches on wing tips.

NAME: AMERICAN ROBIN (*Turdus migratorius*)
STATE BIRD OF: CONNECTICUT, MICHIGAN, WISCONSIN
COLOR IT: Dark gray head, nape, back, rump and tail, lighter gray under wings. White throat with black pattern, broken white streak over eye, yellow beak, brown legs, reddish-orange breast and belly.

NAME: WILLOW PTARMIGAN (*Lagopus lagopus*)
STATE BIRD OF: ALASKA
COLOR IT: Red comb, white wings, legs and feet, red-brown head and neck. Red-brown sides with white pattern. Dark brown back, rump and tail with white pattern.

NAME: BROWN PELICAN (*Pelecanus occidentalis*)
STATE BIRD OF: LOUISIANA
COLOR IT: White head, bluish around the eye, black patch between the eye and bill, light brown beak with dark brown pouch, red-brown nape, gray-brown body.

NAME: NENE OR HAWAIIAN GOOSE (*Branta sandvicensis*)
STATE BIRD OF: HAWAII
COLOR IT: Black head and beak, orange cheek patch, black tail, legs and feet. White neck with dark brown pattern. White breast and belly with brown scale pattern. Dark brown wings with white streaks.

NAME: COMMON LOON (*Gavia immer*)
STATE BIRD OF: MINNESOTA
COLOR IT: Black head and neck with patterned white ring. White breast. Black and white patterns over entire body.

NAME: RUFFED GROUSE (*Bonasa umbellus*)
STATE BIRD OF: PENNSYLVANIA
COLOR IT: Light brown head with white eye patches, yellow beak, black neck ruff. Light brown fan tail with dark brown pattern and edged with white and black. Light brown body, wings and rump with white or dark brown patterns.

NAME: BALD OR AMERICAN EAGLE (*Haliaeetus leucocephalus*)
NATIONAL BIRD OF: UNITED STATES OF AMERICA
COLOR IT: White head, neck and tail, yellow beak, legs and feet. Entire body dark brown with lighter brown under wings.

Educational Coloring Books and
STORY CASSETTES

The only non-fiction coloring book/cassette packages available! The cassettes are not read-alongs. Rather, the educational factual information in the coloring book is utilized and enhanced to create exciting stories. Sound, music, and professional narration stimulate interest and promote reading. Children can color and listen, color alone, or simply listen to the cassette. We are proud to offer these quality products at a reasonable price.

DISPLAY RACKS AVAILABLE. INDIVIDUALLY PACKAGED.

YOUR CHOICE OF 48 TITLES

"ISBN (INTERNATIONAL STANDARD BOOK NUMBER) PREFIX ON ALL BOOKS AND CASSETTES: 0-86545-

- No. 082-X DINOSAURS
- No. 083-8 Prehistoric SEA LIFE
- No. 084-6 Prehistoric BIRDS
- No. 085-4 CAVE MAN
- No. 086-2 Prehistoric FISH
- No. 087-0 Prehistoric MAMMALS
- No. 097-8 Count/Color DINOSAURS
- No. 089-7 PLAINS INDIANS
- No. 090-0 NORTHEAST INDIANS
- No. 091-9 NORTHWEST INDIANS
- NO. 092-7 SOUTHEAST INDIANS
- No. 093-5 SOUTHWEST INDIANS
- No. 094-3 CALIFORNIA INDIANS
- No. 153-2 ESKIMOS
- No. 152-4 COWBOYS
- No. 150-8 COLONIES
- No. 151-6 PIONEERS
- No. 154-0 FARM ANIMALS
- No. 095-1 DOLLS
- No. 096-X ANIMAL ALPHABET
- No. 160-5 CATS
- No. 161-3 DOGS
- No. 162-1 HORSES
- No. 159-1 BIRDS
- No. 147-8 PENGUINS
- No. 098-6 STATE BIRDS
- No. 163-X STATE FLOWERS
- No. 100-1 MAMMALS
- No. 101-X REPTILES
- No. 158-3 POISONOUS SNAKES
- No. 102-8 CATS OF THE WILD
- No. 103-6 ENDANGERED SPECIES
- No. 157-5 PRIMATES
- No. 104-4 ANIMAL GIANTS
- No. 148-6 ATLANTIC FISH
- No. 149-4 PACIFIC FISH
- No. 105-2 SHARKS
- No. 106-0 WHALES
- No. 107-9 DEEP-SEA FISH
- No. 108-7 DOLPHINS
- No. 109-5 AIRCRAFT
- No. 110-9 SPACE CRAFT
- No. 111-7 SPACE EXPLORERS
- No. 112-5 PLANETS
- No. 113-3 COMETS
- No. 114-1 ROCKETS
- No. 155-9 TRANSPORTATION
- No. 156-7 SHIPS

ALL BOOK CASSETTE PACKAGES **$4.98** EACH

LISTEN AND COLOR
LIBRARY ALBUMS

6 Educational Coloring Books Book/Story Cassettes
In a plastic storage case

We have gathered cassettes and books of related subject matter into individual library albums. Each album will provide a new, in-depth, and lasting learning experience. They are presented in a beautiful binder that will store and protect your collection for years.

We also invite you to pick 6 titles of your chosing and create your own CUSTOM ALBUM.

LIBRARY ALBUMS **$34.95** EACH

CHOOSE ANY LIBRARY ALBUM LISTED, OR SELECT TITLES FOR YOUR CUSTOM ALBUM

No. 088-9 Prehistoric Life
Dinosaurs
Prehistoric Sea Life
Prehistoric Fish
Prehistoric Birds
Prehistoric Mammals
Cave Man

No. 116-8 American Indian
Plains Indians
Northeast Indians
Northwest Indians
Southeast Indians
Southwest Indians
California Indians

No. 164-8 Oceans & Seas
Atlantic Fish
Pacific Fish
Sharks
Whales
Deep-Sea Fish
Dolphins

No. 117-6 Air & Space
Aircraft
Space Craft
Space Explorers
Planets
Comets
Rockets

No. 165-6 Americana
Colonies
Cowboys
Pioneers
State Flowers
State Birds
Endangered Species

No. 166-4 Animal Libr #1
Poisonous Snakes
Reptiles
Animal Giants
Mammals.
Cats of the Wild
Primates

No. 167-2 Animal Libr. #2
Prehistoric Mammals
Birds
Farm Animals
Endangered Species
Animal Alphabet
State Birds

No. 168-0 Young Students
Animal Alphabet
Counting & Coloring Dinosaurs
Dolls
Dogs
Cats
Horses

No. 170-2 New Titles Library
Eskimos
State Flowers
Penguins
Atlantic Fish
Pacific Fish
Farm Animals

No. 169-9 Custom Library
WE INVITE YOU TO PICK 6 TITLES OF YOUR CHOSING AND CREATE YOUR OWN CUSTOM LIBRARY.